Insiders

Written by
Chris Powling

Illustrated by Martin Remphry

CHAPTER 1

Rio was at the end of the garden again, snooping. This wasn't easy on a cold winter's night. If he perched on the rain barrel, though, and balanced himself between the fence and the tool shed, he could just about see Mr Emmett ...

Luckily, the old man hadn't drawn the curtains in his upstairs room next door. There he was, framed in the brightly-lit window. He had an easel in front of him, a palette in the crook of his arm and a long, thin brush in his hand – just like a proper artist, in fact. But what kind of proper artist wears a collar and tie while he works?

And what was he painting, anyway?

It was impossible to tell from here. But this didn't stop Rio from stretching a little further to see – perhaps more than was strictly sensible for a kid already on tiptoe.

Oh dear ...

Leaping clear, he was hardly touched himself, but the commotion as the barrel fell over, flooding the lawn with water as it rolled down the garden path, sounded deafening to Rio. People would think it was just a cat fight, he told himself hopefully. Or maybe a fox.

Meanwhile, as he rubbed his bruises, he saw Mr Emmett hadn't noticed a thing. He was still up there in the window, dab-dab-dabbing at his canvas as if nothing at all had happened.

Silly old fool.

Limping a bit, Rio hurried indoors. He hung up his coat in the lobby and made straight for the sitting room in case he'd been missed. His mother, and his big sister Felicity, were deep in conversation – except Mum was doing all the talking as usual.

Fliss seemed to be trying hard not to scream. When he heard what Mum was saying, Rio almost screamed himself.

She was going to be killed … again.

Her voice was husky as she broke the news. 'They'll strike without mercy, darlings. I'm worth more to them dead than alive, you know. Think of the fabulous publicity they'll get!'

'Mum, that's what you said last time,' Fliss groaned. 'And they made your part even bigger in the end.'

'That was then,' said Mum, darkly. 'This is now … and our ratings have been iffy for months. If they can boost them by finishing me off, they won't hesitate for a second. The whole series may be at stake, remember. My death could save everyone's job.'

'How?' Fliss frowned.

'Because it'll make such an impact, darling. The viewing figures will go through the roof. INSIDERS is a national institution, remember. It's been adored by millions of viewers for more than a quarter of a century. All it needs to recover its popularity is the sacrifice of one of its principal characters …' Mum gave a long, tragic sigh.

Leaning back on the sofa, her face deathly pale from the strain of it all, she let the script she'd been reading drop from her hand. Fliss picked it up from the carpet, found the right place again, and handed it back. 'I understand all that, Mum,' she said. 'What I meant was … how will they kill you?'

'Good question,' nodded Rio. 'If it's going to save the whole programme, it'll have to be pretty dramatic.'

'Some sort of horrible accident, maybe?' Fliss suggested.

'Or a long, lingering illness?'

'A murder, perhaps, all gory and agonising?'

'Suicide, even?'

Mum stared at them suspiciously. It was one of the beady-eyed, looking-down-her-nose sort of stares made famous by Rosie Ramone, the character she'd been playing in INSIDERS since long before they were born. 'Are you two sending me up?' she asked, coldly.

'Us?' Fliss said.

'No way,' said Rio. 'This is crucial, Mum. Rosie Ramone isn't just an ordinary INSIDER, after all … she's been there right from the beginning!'

'Like forever,' said his sister.

'Not quite forever,' Mum sniffed. 'That's simply how it feels to everyone because Rosie has such … such presence.'

'Hold on a minute,' said Rio, clicking his fingers. 'There's one way you can pop your clogs that's perfectly natural and believable. Also, it'll keep you on screen a few months longer, Mum. You wouldn't even have to act very much.'

'What way is that, darling?'

'Old age,' Rio said.

Mum sat very still.

Her face had the look of someone who's swallowed a wasp – another expression Rosie Ramone had made her own. Slowly, she got to her feet. Pausing a moment to make sure she had her children's full attention, she flung one end of her crimson pashmina over her shoulder and stalked from the room.

Rio winked at his sister. 'Well, I guess we'd better take that as a no, then.'

''fraid so, bruv.' Grinning, they smacked hands in a high five.

Mum was always like this when her contract came up for renewal. Once she'd signed the next one, her moaning and groaning miraculously shifted – to all the wonderful roles she'd be missing now she was tied down hand and foot.

'Actors!' said Fliss, with a grin. 'They're as nutty as fruitcakes, all of them!' She gazed fondly round the living room.

At first glance, it seemed abnormally cluttered – too many books and pictures for one thing. But these were far from haphazard. The books were mostly dramas and screenplays, and the pictures weren't really pictures at all. Instead, here were carefully-framed posters and studio portraits, cast lists and movie stills, publicity material and assorted clippings from the press. Mum's friends and colleagues from INSIDERS were the main subjects, naturally.

But the star was Rosie Ramone. Wherever you sat, you couldn't help catching sight of her – viewed in close-up, medium and long-shot from every possible angle. Even the screen saver, as it floated on the ancient PC in the corner, showed Rosie accepting an award. 'Yeah, actors are truly weird,' Rio nodded. 'But painters are just the same if you ask me. I've been watching Mr Emmett next door, Fliss. Night after night he's up there in his back bedroom dabbing away – and he can't be a real artist.'

'Why not?'

'What, dressed in an old suit and waistcoat? He ought to be wearing a smock or something.'

'You reckon?'

'Of course he should. From the look of him, he splashes more paint on his clothes than he does on his picture. He's got this glint in his eye, too, as if he's in some sort of trance.'

'You could see the glint in his eye?'

'Well … not quite,' said Rio. 'But I bet I would have done if I'd been a bit closer.'

Fliss wrinkled her nose disapprovingly. As she eyed her little brother, she looked rather Rosie-ish herself. 'Rio, that's awful,' she told him. 'What you've been doing is … well, it's spying, isn't it?'

'Spying?'

'Isn't that how it sounds to you?'

'No way, Fliss! If you've got an old guy like Mr Emmett next door, you're supposed to look out for him, aren't you? In case he gets sick, I mean. Or falls over and hurts himself. He could lie there for days, undiscovered.'

'And that's the reason you're doing it?'

'Why else?' said Rio, airily. It was one of his reasons, anyway.

Okay, so he was also getting in a bit of practice – to be a proper detective one day, perhaps. Or maybe a drugs-buster for Customs and Excise. Best of all, if things worked out the way he wanted, he'd become an investigative journalist like their dad who'd been working in America since he and Mum split up. You had to start somewhere, after all. And it wasn't the sort of thing they taught you in school.

Besides, there really was something eerie about Mr Emmett. He wasn't just eccentric, he was like someone left over from another age. Now Mum had moved them from their smart apartment in the city centre to a stuffy suburb like this one, it was simply common sense to check out an oddball who lived so close.

Well, wasn't it?

CHAPTER 2

'So it was you all along, then …'

'Could've been.'

'Come on, 'fess up. We're mates, aren't we?'

Rio groaned and gave in. 'Okay, Denzel. It was me falling off the rain barrel, actually. Most of the water had spilled out before I hit the ground but half the street must have heard it.'

'Nah,' said Denzel. 'It wasn't that loud.'

'Loud enough for you to hear, though.'

'Our flat overlooks your garden, doesn't it? Besides, I know what you're up to. I kind of expect strange noises.'

'Great,' Rio said. So much for his skills as a snooper.

Maybe this was a waste of time too – huddling themselves behind a tree on the pavement opposite Mr Emmett's house. Luckily, Denzel was the kind of kid you could trust, whether something happened or not. Denzel was cool. He wasn't in the least bit star-struck at having Rosie Ramone as a neighbour, unlike his parents. For him, the mysterious Mr Emmett was much more interesting.

'And you reckon he was painting a picture up there in his room?' Denzel asked. 'Like that Dutch guy? The one who chopped off his ear after he'd drawn all those daffodils, I mean.'

'Sunflowers,' Rio said.

'Mr Emmett was painting sunflowers?'

'No,' said Rio, patiently. 'The Dutch guy was – the one who chopped off his ear.'

'Whatever,' Denzel shrugged. 'They both sound bonkers to me. Maybe all painters are like that. Next time we see Mr E I'm going to count his ears very carefully. He might turn out to be Dutch.'

'Or a genius, Den.'

'Another Van Gogh, you mean,' Denzel suggested.

Rio blinked in surprise. 'That's the guy, yes. How did you remember his name all of a sudden?'

'Art and Culture.'

'What?'

'Crops up regularly, every Thursday, down at the local with Mum and Dad. They never miss the Pub Quiz if they can help it. We practise at home all the time. Your mum got a mention last week, Rio.'

'Did she?'

'In Media and Entertainment. They had to name the only actor in history who's become world-famous despite only playing one role. *Rosie Ramone*, Dad said straightaway. He was really teed off when they told him he'd got it wrong.'

'But it isn't wrong,' Rio said.

'It is, you know. That's not her real name, is it? It's the name of the character she plays. Rosie Leverton was the right answer. Everyone loses a mark there, apparently. They get the two confused.'

'So does Mum,' said Rio, dryly. Sometimes he got confused himself wondering if he was Rio Leverton or Rio Ramone.

Rio sighed and took another peek across the road – making sure most of him was still hidden by the tree. He and Denzel had been staking the house out for half an hour now. It seemed the perfect place for an elderly, absent-minded old gent who lived like a hermit and wore a paint-stained suit most of the time.

'Looks a bit neglected, doesn't it?' Denzel said. 'But the old boy can't be short of dosh if he can afford to live by himself in a house that size, Rio. He could easily sell it for megabucks if he was short of cash.'

'I suppose he could …'

'Of course he could. Prices are going through the roof in this area. Houses are changing hands all the time. It's called "gentrification". People are even buying up leftover council flats like ours.'

'Maybe Mr Emmett likes it the way it is.'

'Yeah?'

Actually, Rio doubted this himself. With its tall, matching bay windows and stone front porch, its built-to-last fittings and handsome sweep of a driveway, Mr Emmett's house was practically the twin of their own next door – 'a gem of the Early Victorian era' the estate agent had told them.

There the comparison ended, though. The old man's property was solid enough, admittedly. But there was nothing 'gentrified' about it. It had the drab and anonymous air of a building not meant to be noticed.

Denzel lowered his voice to a whisper. 'Shall we take a look round the back, Rio?'

'We'd better not, Den.'

'Why? What kind of a detective are you? That's what we're here for, isn't it? A bit of reconnaissance? It's what detectives do.'

'Yes, but ...' Rio broke off.

That's exactly what they were there for. Earlier on, he'd used the very same word to tempt Denzel into a bit of snooping. What he hadn't quite realised was how far his new friend would be willing to go.

Warily, he glanced over his shoulder. Already dusk was deepening the nooks and crannies of the afternoon. It wasn't yet dark, though. The street was still mostly in daylight and the sky above them remained a delicate, wintry blue. If they didn't hang about, maybe they'd be back indoors before nightfall.

He licked his lips. 'We'll have to be quick then ...'

Instantly, Denzel was off like a whippet.

Rio had to sprint after him at once or risk having to make the whole trip on his own. Shoulder to shoulder, they scurried over the road, across the driveway, and through a gate, which was standing half open. Soon they were tiptoeing along the overgrown path at the side of the house. They passed an outside loo, a set of dustbins, and a kitchen door with old-fashioned glass panels. No light seemed to be shining inside.

There was no one in the rear garden, either. It looked just as nondescript as the rest of the house. Rio nearly laughed out loud with relief. That's till he glanced up at the bedroom window. He was much closer than he'd been last night – so close, in fact, he had to take a step backwards for a proper view. When he recognised who was standing there, he gasped in astonishment.

Denzel caught Rio's arm and pointed. 'Hey!' he exclaimed. 'Do you see who that is?'

'Yes,' said Rio, faintly. But he still couldn't quite believe it.

Mum often boasted how truthful INSIDERS was. In her opinion, the twists and turns of its storyline simply mirrored the way life itself chopped and changed. Only the boldest of the programme's scriptwriters would have offered a turnaround like this, though.

For the person at the window, propped against the sill with her back to the glass, was his own sister Fliss.

CHAPTER 3

Mr Emmett could draw all right. Fliss saw that straightaway. With a few flicks of his brush, the painting on the easel seemed to be developing like a photograph in front of her.

No, not like a photograph.

In a photograph you get useless bits as well. Here, he was only including the essentials. You could tell at once what was important from its shape and texture and position. Fliss stared in amazement. How could a bit of fidgeting with your fingers make such a difference? 'Hey, that looks like my brother!' she exclaimed.

'Perched on a rain barrel,' said Mr Emmett. 'Well, he's trying to perch ...'

And, suddenly, there was the barrel – already in mid-tip – its water gushing out beneath Rio's scrabbling feet.

'You've got it exactly right,' Fliss laughed. 'That's the way Rio described it. How do you do that?'

'Practice, my dear. Lots and lots of practice.' Mr Emmett looked up from the easel.

With his paint-spattered clothes and mop of white hair, he should have been a scary figure, she realised. But his eyes, grey and thoughtful, were the kindest she'd ever seen. They were peering at her now from beneath a lifted eyebrow. 'Er … forgive me for asking,' he said. 'But haven't I seen you somewhere before?'

'Well, I've lived next door for the last three months.'

'As long as that, is it?'

'It must be … maybe longer. And you've seen my brother out in the garden, obviously. People are always saying how much alike we are. Also we take after Mum, of course.'

Fliss sighed as she spoke.

Sooner or later the talk always got round to Mum.

Mr Emmett frowned as if he wasn't quite sure on that point. 'Is she the lady in the dark glasses?' he asked. 'The one who's always wearing a headscarf when she goes out?'

'That's her, yes.'

'She's a creature of habit like me, then.' Again came his gentle smile.

Fliss smiled, too. For once, it seemed, Mum's fame wouldn't be hijacking the entire conversation. The old man hadn't even heard of her. Or was he just being polite? 'Mum's name is Rosie,' she told him, carefully. 'Rosie Leverton to be exact.'

'That's a lovely name,' he nodded. 'So you must be Fliss Leverton, then. And your brother, the young acrobat, is called …'

'Rio.'

'Sorry?'

'Rio … like the footballer?'

'If you say so, my dear.' No flicker of recognition there, either.

Fliss nearly let out a whoop of delight. It wasn't often, these days, she had the chance to be someone in her own right. Usually, she found herself typecast as The Daughter of Rosie Ramone. Maybe moving here had been one of Mum's better decisions.

Like this surprise visit to Mr Emmett?

Speaking for herself, she didn't regret suggesting it to Mum at all. She'd taken an instant liking to this shy old man with his quiet voice and charming manners. And at least she'd got in ahead of Rio. Her brother was such a busybody sometimes – especially now he was so keen to impress his new friend Denzel. It was just like him to turn Mr Emmett into some kind of surveillance operation.

Actually, the old man was lonely.

That was obvious, wasn't it? All this art stuff looked completely genuine to Fliss. Maybe he really was a proper painter. But it was also the perfect hobby for someone with a lot of time on his hands. 'Did you do *all* these pictures?' she asked.

'Every one of them, Fliss. What you're looking at here is more than five years' solid work.'

'Work?' said Fliss in surprise.

'You don't think painting is work, then?'

'Yes ... yes, of course!' said Fliss, hastily. 'But it's been so much fun this afternoon.'

'Oh, it can be fun too. Sometimes, when your brain and your brush and your eye team up, it feels like the best fun in the world. It's as if you can transfer what's in your head straight on to the canvas.'

'That doesn't always happen?'

'Dear me, no ...'

'What do you do on the bad days?'

'You carry on as if they were good days. And sometimes, if you concentrate hard enough, that's how they turn out.'

Fliss nodded at that. She'd heard Mum make much the same point about acting. Only amateurs needed to get themselves 'in the right mood' to deliver a good performance, she'd always sniff. A professional simply gets on with the job.

Was Mr Emmett a professional, then?

Fliss still wasn't sure. Does a professional really balance his easel on an ancient mahogany dressing table and cram the battered wardrobe that matches it – its doors gaping open – with tins and tubes and other painterly oddments? On the other hand, there were piles of canvasses everywhere, all with their faces turned away from her so it was impossible to tell which were blank, which were finished, and which at some stage in-between. 'May I take a peek?' Fliss asked.

'At one of my paintings?'

'If you don't mind, Mr Emmett.'

He hesitated.

As he gazed round the studio, a cloud seemed to pass over his long, thin face. He tried to smile but somewhere between his lips and his eyes this never quite took hold. 'Please yourself,' he said, gruffly.

'Which one shall I look at, then?'

'Any one you like.' He shrugged and turned to the window.

Fliss bit her lip, embarrassed. She wished she'd never asked. But she'd have to go through with it now. She chose a medium-sized canvas, separate from the rest, which leant against the corner of the wardrobe. Carefully, in case it might still be wet, she swivelled it so it was face-outwards catching the light.

As she stepped back, she shut her eyes.

When she opened them, she was in a different world. Oh, there was nothing alien about it – nothing weird or freakish. The scene was almost homely, in fact. It showed a street in the city centre, viewed from a distance, but with every detail starkly clear. Didn't she recognise these shops, these buildings? The people seemed so real she felt she almost recognised them.

Somehow, life had never looked quite like this, though. Not so sharp or so … personal.

Yes, that was the word. Even the boring bits – the bits so ordinary and everyday that you didn't notice them normally – seemed completely and utterly personal. Was this what happened when your brain and your brush and your eye teamed up?

Fliss let out a hiss of admiration. 'That's the city centre, isn't it?' she asked.

'Well spotted,' said Mr Emmett. 'Mind you, I was painting it how it was when I was a boy. There's a lot more traffic around nowadays. And the shops are posher, too.'

'It hasn't changed that much, though.'

'No, not that much.'

In a way, it hadn't changed at all.

What he'd caught was the bare bones of his subject, not just the surface detail. Actually, it was a child's vision of the world, Fliss realised. Yet it was hard to imagine anyone except a grown-up being able to paint as skilfully as this.

Mr Emmett gave the gentlest possible cough. 'So you like it then, do you?' he asked.

'Yes, I do ... honestly I do.'

'Borrow it, then.'

'What?'

'You can have it "on loan", Fliss. To see if you still like it once you get to know it better.'

'Are you sure?' Fliss gasped.

She could see at once that he was.

A little later, the studio being so cluttered, they had to change places. This gave Mr Emmett the elbow room he needed to parcel-up the painting properly, in bubble wrap and cardboard, so it would be safe on its long and arduous journey next door. Fliss was amazed at all the trouble he took. While he fussed with scissors and sticky tape, she stood with her back to the bedroom window, oblivious of the fading sky behind her and the darkening garden below.

That's when Rio and Denzel saw her, of course.

CHAPTER 4

Fliss could see she was in disgrace. Her brother was sprawled on the sofa, stony-faced, and his friend Denzel wouldn't meet her eyes at all. Instead, he gazed open-mouthed round their living room as if stunned by this shrine to INSIDERS.

Why were they so cross with her?

Eventually, she couldn't stand it any longer. 'Rio,' she said. 'If it's not too much trouble, do you mind telling me why you're both in such a foul mood?'

'You can't work it out, Fliss?'

'No, I can't. And I'm fed up with trying to guess, okay?'

'So what's that thing over there?'

'The parcel?'

'Boom-boom,' said Rio.

She'd left it leaning against the computer table, still protected by Mr Emmett's packaging. Fliss felt her cheeks burning. 'Oh, that …' she said.

'Yes … that,' said Rio. 'Looks like a painting to me. A next-door type of painting to be exact. Call me suspicious but it makes me think of an old guy in a messy suit.' He was glaring at her now.

Suddenly, she understood. 'You were snooping again, weren't you,' she said. 'And you saw me up at the window.'

'Might've done.'

'Yes, you did … you were lurking out in the garden, pretending to be detectives. And now I've wrecked your little game by finding out the truth – that he's just a shy and lonely old man who's nutty about drawing and painting.'

'Did you tell Mum about your visit, then?'

'About calling on Mr Emmett? Of course I did – before I'd even knocked on his door, actually. How about you, Rio?'

'What?'

'Did you tell her you and Denzel were planning to sniff out all of our neighbour's secrets?'

Rio shifted awkwardly on the sofa. They both knew how Mum felt about snoopers. As the star of a TV soap, she was on permanent red alert for reporters from the press. It was one of the reasons why they'd moved away from the city centre. Also it was one of the reasons, they suspected, why she and Dad had finally agreed to live apart.

Rio considered this carefully before he answered. 'Okay,' he said, with a shrug. 'Let's call it quits, Fliss. But next time you pay him a visit can we come with you?'

'Yeah, we want to see the genius at work,' said Denzel.

'It's a deal,' said Fliss. 'Mr Emmett is so keen to paint my portrait, I'm sure he wouldn't mind if you two tagged along.'

'He wants to paint you?' said Rio in disbelief.

'Amazingly enough, yes!'

Denzel cleared his throat, politely. While the two of them had been bickering, his gaze had settled on Mr Emmett's parcel by the computer. He gave it a nod. 'Can't see much point in having him paint you or anyone else if he isn't much cop as an artist, right? So why don't we check him out?'

'Go ahead,' Fliss said. She watched as they struggled to open the parcel.

Once the picture could be lifted clear of its coverings, they stood it under one of the spotlights for close viewing. Of course, it was only oil paint on canvas – not even properly framed as yet.

So why did it cast such a spell?

Scowling, Rio did his best to be critical. 'Not exactly well drawn, is it?' he sniffed. 'They're not much more than blobs, those people. And the buildings all round them are sort of sketchy. The whole thing's got a cartoony feel to it.'

'Picasso did that,' Denzel said.

'Eh?'

'His pictures sometimes have a cartoony feel to them. He could draw very realistically but sometimes he chose not to.'

'You think Mr Emmett is another Picasso?'

'How would I know? I'm not an art expert. Besides, their style's completely different – his and Picasso's, I mean. All I'm saying is that there's more than one way you can paint a picture. And this is Mr Emmett's way.'

'Right ...'

Rio stared at the picture even harder. They all did.

And the harder they stared, the more they seemed to see in Mr Emmett's brush-stroke figures and simplified scenery. It was as if his picture made them look at the world through his eyes instead of their own.

Soon they were lost completely in his vision of the city's main street as it had been more than half a century ago. When the door of the sitting room suddenly crashed open, they jumped as if they'd been shot. 'What's up, Mum?' yelped Fliss in alarm.

'Don't worry, darling. It's all under control more or less. There's no need for anyone to panic.' She was in Rosie mode, of course.

With one hand upraised, she steadied herself against the door frame. With the other, she clutched at her throat. From her lips came a tearing, choking sob. Even for Mum this was over the top.

Fliss shot a glance at her brother. 'Something's happened!' she exclaimed in alarm.

'Is it news about your contract?' Rio asked.

'Darlings ...' Mum seemed to be fighting for breath. When she spoke again, there were tears in her eyes. 'Darlings,' she declared. 'I've only got three months to live.'

'Three months to live?' gasped Denzel. 'That's awful!'

'She's talking about INSIDERS, Den.'

'Oh, sorry ...' Denzel dropped his eyes,

embarrassed.

It was an easy mistake to make, though. Especially the way Mum explained it. She did this standing up, like a piece to the camera, as if millions of viewers were hanging on every word.

The Head of Series Drama, Hal McRory, had made the decision to kill her off, just as she'd predicted, as part of the Easter ratings battle. In his estimation, half the nation at the very least would stay indoors to watch the end of Rosie Ramone. Mum's agent, Miriam Markham, had phoned with the news. 'It's nothing personal, sweetie,' she'd cooed. 'Strictly a matter of viewing figures, I understand.'

'I know how it works,' Mum had said.

'And I've negotiated a wonderful deal for you – a whole year's salary for only three months' filming provided you sign the contract immediately.'

'Sign my own death certificate, you mean?'

'Now don't be like that, dear. You'll be on every front page in the land, remember. And you've had a very good run for your money, you've got to agree. Thirty years in the nation's top television soap is a truly remarkable achievement. How old were you when you made your first appearance on screen?'

'I was six.'

'Seven, actually,' Miriam had reminded her. 'Six was the age of Rosie Ramone at the time.' Mum reported all this in detail.

Over and over again, naturally.

She played herself and her agent, in role, to make sure the three of them understood the full extent of the tragedy. Afterwards, with eyelids a flutter and her face a deathly pale, she subsided on to the sofa with a low, lingering moan. She seemed to be half-rehearsing already for Rosie's last moments alive.

It was almost a relief when the phone rang. Hal McRory himself was on the line. Would Mum come and see him as soon as possible, he begged, so they could discuss the situation face to face as old friends should? 'You see how it is in television?' Mum groaned as she put down the handset. 'I'm being assassinated by an old, old friend!'

But she left straightaway, they noticed.

The room was strangely quiet when she'd gone. Was it just their imagination, or did the photographs of Rosie all round them look ghostly and outdated already? 'Maybe we should take them down,' said Rio, gloomily. 'Or at least turn them to face the wall.'

'Won't that make it worse?' Fliss sighed.

'But she'll get other parts, won't she?' asked Denzel. 'She's been famous for years and years. Even if INSIDERS has dumped her, she's not going to sink without trace!'

'Most former soap-stars do, Den.'

'Mum's brilliant as Rosie Ramone,' Fliss said. 'But even she's not sure how good she'd be at playing someone else. That's why she's so actor-ish when she's not in front of the cameras. It's her way of keeping her confidence up.'

'Blimey! I'm glad my ma and pa do ordinary jobs!'

'Lucky them,' said Fliss, standing up.

'Where are you going, sis?'

'To put Mr Emmett's picture back in its packing. You know, Mum didn't even notice it was here! Anyway, we'd better keep it safe and sound till we take it back to him.'

'But he's lent it to you, hasn't he? Why return it so soon?'

'In case it's really valuable, Rio. Suppose

we had a break-in – or somehow it got damaged?'

Standing there, in the doorway, she looked more than ever like a younger, less showy version of her mother. Rio stared at the painting thoughtfully. 'Come to think of it,' he said, 'I wouldn't mind finding out what it's worth.'

'No problem,' said Denzel.

'What?'

'There's a really posh gallery down in the city centre. You know the one I mean? It's only ever got one thing in its window – a picture or an old pot or a fancy bit of sculpture.'

'And there's never any price tag …'

'That's the one, Rio. Dead classy, it is. They say people even come down from London to see what it's got on display. I bet someone in that place can give us the low-down on Mr E.'

'You reckon?'

'Got to be worth a bus ride, hasn't it? For all we know, we could be looking after something that's worth millions!'

'Yeah!' Rio's eyes lit up at the thought of another investigation.

Fliss bit her lip, uneasily. It was hard to disagree with their reasoning ... except for the sneaky feeling, deep inside her, that this was just another way of snooping on a harmless old man whose hobby had taken over his life. She'd never get Rio and Denzel to see it like that, though. And at least a trip to the gallery would take their minds off INSIDERS for a while.

Besides, she was curious about the painting herself.

CHAPTER 5

Luckily, it was late-night shopping in the city centre so there was no need for them to rush. Less luckily, every bus on its way there was already standing-room only. Their arms ached from protecting the painting by the time they reached the gallery.

It was a bigger place, and grander, than they'd expected. But Denzel had been right about the window. Most of it was draped in dark, heavy-textured velvet – apart from a small oblong seascape propped on a miniature easel. It looked at least a couple of centuries old. 'And it's nothing like Mr Emmett's painting,' said Rio, nervously.

'They've got other paintings inside,' said Fliss.

'Are they like Mr Emmett's?'

'Can't see from here.'

'Only one way to find out,' Denzel said. 'Let's go in and take a peek. I'll do the talking, okay?'

He was already opening the door.

It shut itself behind them with an expensive-sounding hiss. The hustle and bustle of the city, on the other side of the glass, suddenly seemed a million miles away.

So did Mr Emmett's back bedroom.

These pictures, all seascapes in gilt frames as far as they could see, gave an impression of proper artists, dressed in proper artists' clothes, maybe with an ear missing here and there. Every aspect of the gallery – the temperature, the lighting, the décor – had a soothing and professional feel to it. Even Denzel was impressed. 'Hey,' he whispered. 'This joint's serious!'

'May I help you?' came a voice. This was serious, too.

She was about Mum's age, they estimated. But in her dark, tailored suit and crisp white blouse, she looked altogether more steely. On her lapel was a small, discreet nametag, which read *Louise Marshall – Director of Acquisitions*. 'Have you brought something to show me?' she enquired.

'This picture, miss.' Denzel said.

'You've done it yourself?' Ms Marshall smiled warily.

Perhaps this was the first time she'd ever encountered a black kid, in scruffy denims, with a painting under his arm. Coolly, Denzel smiled back as if he'd encountered millions of people like her. 'Not me, miss,' he said. 'Personally, I'm into computer graphics. This is by somebody else. But we reckon you might find it interesting.'

'Let's hope so.'

'Don't mess up the cardboard, please. We'll be taking it home again on the bus.'

'I'll open it carefully, I promise.'

'Thanks,' Denzel said. He held out the parcel.

She took it, still smiling politely, though its weight was clearly a surprise to her. 'It's on canvas, isn't it?' she said.

'I think so, miss.'

'Someone's wrapped it professionally, too.'

'Mr Emmett,' Fliss told her.

'JK Emmett?'

'We're neighbours of his,' said Rio. 'He lent this painting to my sister for a while and we decided to find out a bit more about it. Why, have you heard of him?'

'He's famous,' added Denzel, quickly.

Ms Marshall was staring hard at them now. Slowly, she let out a deep breath. 'Well, there's only one artist called JK Emmett that I know of. And a few years ago he was on the brink of becoming very well known indeed. Shall we take a look?'

'Go ahead,' said Denzel.

'Thank you.'

She lifted the parcel on to a nearby table, flicked on a spotlight, and from somewhere produced a sharp, stubby knife. She cut the heavy-duty tape round the edges with neat, straight strokes so the whole package could be reassembled quite easily.

Gently, she pulled the canvas clear of its wrappings. Then she stood it where it was fully lit.

Her response was almost immediate. 'Oh, yes …' she murmured. 'Yes … yes. This is JK Emmett all right.'

After that no one spoke for a while. They were too busy looking. The city centre, as depicted by JK Emmett, was utterly like itself and nowhere else. At the same time, miraculously, it was like every city centre there's ever been.

Suddenly, Ms Marshall lifted a finger. 'See the greengrocer's shop?' she pointed. 'There, in the middle of the street? Believe it or not, we're standing inside that shop right at this moment! That's how this gallery used to be before any of us here were born!'

'It's like a kid did it,' Rio remarked.

'That's true, yes. It would have to be an amazingly talented kid though … who's somehow had years of art-school training to develop a technique as glorious as this.'

'Plus practice,' said Fliss. 'Plenty of practice.'

'So what's it worth?' Denzel asked. His words seemed to hang in the air.

Unabashed, he grinned broadly. 'Well, that's what we're here for, aren't we. So what would it set me back?'

'It's a fair question,' said Ms Marshall. She frowned, thoughtfully. 'In my opinion, this is probably the best thing JK Emmett has ever done,' she said. 'Off the top of my head, and based on current prices, I'd say it would fetch ten thousand pounds at the very least …'

'That much?' Rio gasped.

'It could be a great deal more. These days, it's hard to assess what a new work by

JK Emmett would fetch on the open market.'

'You've lost me,' Denzel said.

Ms Marshall fingered her nametag. Clearly, she was a little uneasy about talking like this to three kids who'd walked in off the street. Then her eye drifted back to the painting on the table.

It seemed to glow there in the spotlight.

Perhaps it was this that made up her mind. 'Look,' she said. 'I'm sorry to be so stuffy. It's just that Jim Emmett is such a special case. Most of his life he worked at an ordinary, everyday job to support his sick mother. He fitted his painting into whatever time was left over – and there was never very much of that, I'm sorry to say. It was years before anyone recognised his talent.'

'But someone did ... eventually?' prompted Fliss.

'Me,' said Ms Marshall.

'You?'

'He simply arrived here one day ... a quiet, shy-looking man in a baggy old raincoat carrying a portfolio of drawings. I'll never forget it. Even then he had to be coaxed into letting me see them. Of course, I recognised their quality at once. And slowly, over the years, other people began to agree with me. His last exhibition was at this very gallery. By then he had quite a following – including the chairman of a big media company who can't get enough of Jim's paintings. To begin with, the show looked likely to be the personal triumph we'd all been waiting for. Jim richly deserved it, goodness knows.'

'So what went wrong?' Denzel asked.

'A couple of days after the opening, quite unexpectedly, his mother died,' said Ms Marshall. 'The following morning, with Jim still reeling from the shock, one of the London critics – just to be different, I think – published a blistering attack on his work. It was truly vicious. That sometimes happens in the art world, I'm afraid.'

'Sounds like a double whammy to me …'

'For Jim, that's exactly what it was. He'd always been very diffident about his talent and guilty about the time he spent up in his studio away from his mother. Now he was utterly crushed. He wouldn't even show me any more paintings, let alone allow me to sell them. This is the first I've seen for almost five years.'

She shook her head in wonder.

'There are stacks more pictures up in his room,' Fliss said. 'Next, he wants to paint a portrait of me. It'll be something out of the ordinary he says – a project he's been planning for ages.'

'You know, that's not surprising. You've got a very striking face … and so has your brother here. When you first walked in I had the oddest of feelings. It was as if, somehow and somewhere, I'd already met you.'

'It's that kind of face,' said Fliss, hastily. 'Loads of people tell us that, don't they, Rio?'

'All the time,' Rio said.

'Yeah,' said Denzel. 'And loads of people mistake me for Denzel Washington. It's a real pain. Thanks for your trouble, miss. If you can pack up Mr E's painting for us, we'll be going now.'

'You will take great care of it …?'

'Nah, don't suppose we'll bother. Not now we know it's only worth a measly ten thousand quid.'

Ms Marshall blinked. Then she laughed out loud. 'I'm sorry,' she said. 'That was pretty pompous, I agree. Just by coming here, you've given me hope that the career of JK Emmett isn't quite over. He really is someone special, you know. Let me pay for a cab to take you home. I owe you that much for keeping an eye on him.'

'It's a deal,' said Denzel. 'Oh, and I wouldn't mind a business card if you've got one handy.'

'Is that a promise to stay in touch, young man?'

Denzel treated her to his broadest, brightest grin. 'Well, you never know your luck,' he said.

CHAPTER 6

Leaving the gallery, they could hardly believe what had happened. Rio and Denzel hadn't even met Mr Emmett yet, while Fliss herself had only spent a couple of hours in his company. Now, though, thanks to Ms Marshall, they were riding home in style … with what might be a modern masterpiece balanced on their knees.

It was Rio who spoke up first. 'Remember she's a dealer,' he said, warily. 'She'll be in it for the money, I expect.'

'At least she's a local,' said Fliss. 'Not one of those beady-eyed sharpies up in London that Mum's always moaning about.'

'I liked her,' said Denzel.

The other two stared at him.

He pulled a face. 'Okay, so I gave her a bit of a hard time. That's how I sometimes am with people I like. With her, though … well, she seemed genuinely fond of the old guy.'

'That's true.'

'She didn't treat us like kids, either – not really.'

'More like grown-ups,' Rio said.

Travelling by taxi felt pretty grown-up, too.

The ride was over almost too soon. Ahead of them, as they turned the corner into their street, the trees were bare and shadowy under the street lamps – except further along where the shadows suddenly vanished. There, every trunk and paving stone stood out in a blaze of light … or they would have done but for the trucks, the crew cars and the outside broadcast units cluttering the kerbside.

'What's going on here?' the cab driver exclaimed. 'Some kind of circus, is it?'

'Better drop us off,' said Rio.

'We'll walk the rest of the way,' added Fliss. They knew exactly what kind of circus it was.

So did Denzel after they'd explained. 'A press conference?' he said. 'You mean, these guys know about your mum already?'

'The TV company probably told them. It's the start of the publicity build-up. Mum will have discussed this with the PR people. They've sent her home to make a statement, I expect.'

'About her own sacking?'

'That's how they play the game, Den.'

Denzel tightened his grip on the painting. 'Hey, I can't get through the crowd lugging this. Is there some other way into your house?'

'Yes, but they'll have staked it out by now,' Rio said. 'Here, give it to me. At least they know who I am. They've seen Mum defending her little darlings before.' Huddling together, they started for home.

As they approached, the crush of people did pull back a bit, making a path for them. It wasn't that wide a path, though, and still bristled with cameras and microphones. 'How's it feel being orphaned, Fliss?' came a cheery shout.

'Ask me when I am one.'

'You're not worried about your Mum's career, then?'

'Not right now,' said Rio, grimly. 'All that worries us is getting to our own front door without having our eyes poked out.'

'Who are you, kid?' someone asked Denzel. 'A friend of the family, maybe?'

'I'm Rosie Ramone's stand-in.'

'What have you got there, Rio?' a reporter wanted to know. 'A get-well-soon card, is it?'

'It's Rosie's P45,' said one of the cameramen. 'She'll be down at the job centre first thing on Monday.' He was greeted with a roar of laughter.

This faded at once when the front door swung open. There, turning the porch into a sort of stage as she stepped out into the hubbub, was the person they'd come to see.

At first, Rosie said nothing while cameras were hastily angled, lights adjusted and sound levels tuned just so. They knew this was the only chance she'd give them. Her hair, her make-up, and the long folds of the evening cloak she'd draped casually over her shoulders, left no room for hitches of a technical kind.

Finally, she began to speak. She'd pitched her voice perfectly for a cold winter's night in one of the quieter streets of the city. 'Thank you for coming,' she said. 'Since you all know why you're here, let's get straight to the point. You're looking at an insider who's about to become an outsider …'

She paused to let their murmuring die away.

Then, with a flick of her cloak, she continued. 'It's sad, of course – at any rate, it is for me. I first appeared in the series when I was younger than my own son and daughter. INSIDERS has been part of my life for thirty wonderful years. So I admit I'll

be shedding a tear or two when my final
credit rolls ...'

Here came another pause.

This allowed everyone to catch the rough-ish Rosie smile as she turned her head from one side of the crowd to the other.

Suddenly, she winked. 'Please don't forget this is only telly, though. It's not war, or famine, or global catastrophe. All we're talking about is a bit of fun that flickers across a screen in your sitting room. So let's not treat it as a tragedy ...'

'But how will they zap you, Rosie?'

'Yes, what's the plan?'

'Have they got the storyline sorted yet?'

'Aha!' said Rosie, in a voice as clear as a church bell. 'Now that would be telling, wouldn't it ...'

She paused yet again.

Quickly, she glanced left and right over each shoulder. She lifted a warning finger to her lips. She bent forward, like a conspirator, as if only the softest whisper would do.

Then she gave Rosie's trademark giggle. 'Better check out our website, guys. Better still, send an email to INSIDERS with your own suggestions. Who knows, you may come up with a better idea than our writers! Pretty soon, I'll be swapping my on-screen family for my real-life one ... so maybe I should get in some practice right now. Thanks again for coming, darlings. Have a safe journey home. And please don't disturb my lovely neighbours as you leave.'

She ushered Fliss, Rio and Denzel into the house.

Her final wave goodbye, before she pulled the front door shut behind her, was perfectly judged for every front page and news bulletin in the country. She even remembered to blow a smacking kiss that was loud enough to be picked up by the microphones.

What a pro …

There was a ragged cheer from the press pack as they straggled out of the driveway and clambered into their waiting vehicles. Fifteen minutes later, the quiet moonlit street looked as safe and dull and respectable as any other in this part of the city.

Inside the house, though, the drama wasn't quite over. Rosie Leverton, or maybe Rosie Ramone, was gazing at a framed black and white photograph which hung at the foot of the stairs. It showed her at Number 10 Downing Street chatting with the Prime Minister. As she stared at herself, and at him, in their elegant evening clothes, her fingers clutched madly at her throat. 'Mum …' Fliss begged, taking her arm.

'It'll be all right, Mum …' Rio promised. But she took not the slightest notice.

In a sudden spasm of activity, she tossed back her hair, uttered a chilling screech of anguish, and flung herself up the stairs with her cloak trailing over the carpet behind her.

Denzel gaped at her retreating figure, open-mouthed. 'What was that all about?' he demanded. 'She was brilliant making her speech a moment ago – totally in charge of things! She had everyone eating out of her hand. Now she's completely gone to pieces!'

'Oh, Denzel,' said Fliss, sadly. 'You don't get it, do you?'

'Get it?'

'There in the porch,' Rio said. 'Didn't you see?'

'See what?'

'That was acting,' Fliss explained.

CHAPTER 7

Mr Emmett hadn't heard a thing.

He propped his brush between the finger and thumb of his palette hand and scratched his head. 'Yesterday evening?' he said. 'Some sort of disturbance outside? What disturbance was that?'

Fliss backtracked at once. 'Just a few noisy visitors,' she said. 'If you didn't hear them, no harm done.'

'Didn't know they were even there, my dear. Mind you, I was probably painting here at the back of the house. What with these thick old walls, and the double glazing, nothing much disturbs me these days. Besides,' he added, tapping his ear, 'often I don't bother switching on my hearing aid after dark!' He grinned apologetically.

From where Fliss sat, he was just a shadow that stood between her and the daylight spilling through the window – a northern light, he'd told her. Apparently, this was the best kind of light for a painter. Only when he turned away, to pick up a brush or a tube of paint, did she catch the fluffy whiteness of his hair or the details of his kindly face.

He'd been working for more than two hours now. Rio and Denzel had been there too – fidgeting in the background with the art materials he'd given them. Fifteen minutes ago, Mr Emmett had finally become weary of their messing about. 'Go downstairs to the sitting room,' the old man had told them, firmly. 'You can watch some television.'

'Any videos, Mr E?' Denzel asked.

'In the cupboard by Mother's armchair.'

'Great!' Rio grinned.

'Cheers!' called Denzel, on his way to the door.

Fliss was glad to be rid of them.

Taking care not to put him off by altering her position, she arched her back to ease out a kink. 'I wonder what they're watching,' she said, idly. 'There's so much rubbish on TV these days.'

'It isn't all bad, my dear.'

'Isn't it?'

'In my experience, television can be a real lifesaver as well – with someone who's sick or lonely, for instance.'

'I suppose so,' said Fliss.

'Mother used to dote on it. Watched it day and night, she did. Took her right out of herself, she always told me. She reckoned it was much better company than a son who wanted to spend all his time painting!'

'I hadn't thought of it like that.'

'Believe me, young lady, I can't thank television enough. Without it, I wouldn't have painted half these pictures. For years and years I didn't even bother to change my clothes when I got home from work. I'd rush straight up here dressed as I was. It's become a bit of a habit, I'm afraid. So you won't hear a word against the box from me!'

'Didn't you ever watch it yourself, then?'

'Sometimes, to keep Mother company. And nowadays I watch it more than ever. It reminds me of her, you see. She was a bossy, crotchety old lady, especially towards the end, but I still miss some of those little ways of hers.' Mr Emmett's eyes twinkled as if his mother had other little ways which he didn't miss much.

Fliss shifted again in her chair.

It was harder work than she'd expected being an artist's model. The worst part was the strain of keeping the same expression on her face so he could get her features exactly right. When she spoke, or coughed, or wrinkled her nose, Mr Emmett never actually grumbled – just paused a moment till she was still again. These pauses were becoming more and more frequent, she realised. Was this because she was getting tired ... or just feeling more and more guilty? Soon, she'd have to speak up.

Then, to her horror, he spoke up for her. It was as if he'd snatched the words from her mouth and re-routed them through his own ... except in a gruff, gentle voice that made her feel even worse. 'Fliss,' he said, hesitantly. 'That painting I lent you yesterday ...'

'The one of the city centre?'

'That's it, yes.'

'Er … what about it, Mr Emmett?'

'Have you … have you shown it to anyone, I wonder?'

Fliss wanted to crawl away. Or maybe just die there and then.

She should never have agreed to taking the picture into town – not without asking Mr Emmett first. The damage was already done, though. So she'd better own up. Nervously, she cleared her throat. 'Well, Rio and Denzel had a good look at it.'

'What did they think?'

'They liked it a lot, Mr Emmett. Honestly, they did. They thought it was so brilliant it deserved an expert opinion.'

'An expert opinion?'

'From the gallery in the city centre, Mr Emmett. In your picture it's still a greengrocer's but nowadays it's a posh art shop. That's where we went to ask their advice.'

Mr Emmett was standing very still. Everything about him seemed to have gone into shock – from the look in his eyes to the whiteness of his knuckles on the paintbrush. Even his face, grey to start with, seemed drained of colour.

Eventually, as if he had to remind himself how to do it, he cleared his throat. 'Would that be ... um, Louise Marshall's gallery?' he asked.

Fliss' cheeks were burning. 'She said she knew you,' she groaned. 'She spoke about you as if she was an old friend of yours. She was really nice to us, too. Even Denzel liked her ...'

'What about the painting?'

'What?'

'The painting, my dear,' said Mr Emmett. 'When you showed it to her, how did she react?'

'Did she like it, do you mean?'

'As an expert, yes.' He smiled, crookedly.

It was a sort of a smile, anyway. Fliss could see how much it cost him – like lifting the heaviest of weights. In her ears buzzed Ms Marshall's remarks about the critic who had hurt him so much after his last exhibition. Suppose she said the wrong thing now? So, with a bit of heavyweight lifting of her own, she smiled back as warmly as she could. 'She was gobsmacked, Mr Emmett!'

'I beg your pardon?'

'Completely gobsmacked,' said Fliss. 'The moment she took it out of its wrappings, she gasped out loud and went into a kind of trance. "Oh, yes," she said. "Yes …"'

'That was all?'

'All?' said Fliss. 'No way! It was hard to shut her up, to tell the truth. There was something about "glorious technique", I remember, and about it being the best thing you'd ever done. She went on to say you deserve to be really famous … stuff like that.' Fliss shrugged and let her voice trail away.

Mr Emmett suddenly straightened up, every inch of him on the alert. 'Hold it right there,' he said, urgently.

'Sorry?'

'Don't move a muscle, Fliss. That expression you've got on your face – I want to capture it as closely as I can.'

'What's so special about it?'

'You look like an actress who's playing a part! Don't worry, my dear. That's not a criticism. On the contrary, it's a part you really believe in. And you're playing it to perfection!'

Fliss wasn't sure if this was good or not.

Mr Emmett seemed quite happy, though. Already he was lost in his painting again, his brow furrowed with concentration and his eyes narrow and squinting as they flicked between Fliss and the portrait of Fliss. He was humming softly to himself. So her confession hadn't gone too badly …

Her mind began to wander.

Mostly, she was asking herself questions. About Mum's career after Rosie Ramone, for instance. About Ms Marshall and her ambitions for Mr Emmett. About this portrait he was painting – that's if it was a portrait. Shouldn't the canvas be propped on the easel longways, she wondered, not sideways as if it were a landscape? Still, he must know what he was doing.

Fliss felt the real world floating away from her. She barely registered the scrape of Mr Emmett's brush against the canvas, the rustle of his paint-stained suit, the muttering under his breath. From somewhere far off, at the very edge of her hearing, she caught the slow, steady notes of a church bell striking noon. It all seemed to be happening inside her, deep in her own mind.

Then she heard two sets of footsteps on the stairs. As Denzel and Rio came in, they didn't say a word. It was Mr Emmett who looked up and spoke first. 'Hello, lads,' he said, cheerily. 'Was there anything interesting on the TV?'

'Well … sort of interesting,' Denzel said.

'More unexpected, really,' said Rio. 'It was something we found in the sitting room, Mr Emmett, next to an old armchair.'

'Ah …' Mr Emmett waved his paintbrush in the air as if in salute to decades of serious viewing. 'If it was facing the television square-on, piled high with cushions, then it was mother's chair,' he chuckled. 'She was so keen on watching in comfort, there was hardly enough space for her! I don't quite follow you, though. What's so unexpected about that?'

'Not the chair itself,' Rio said. 'It was the piles of videotapes in the cupboard beside it which took us by surprise – all neatly labelled and in strict date order. According to our count, not a single episode has been missed for the last thirty years. All the Christmas and Easter Specials are there as well.'

'Respect, man,' grinned Denzel. 'It's the best INSIDERS collection we've ever seen!'

Rio shook his head in awe. 'That mother of yours must have been the programme's Number One Fan!'

'Except for me,' Mr Emmett said.

CHAPTER 8

By now, Denzel was used to the Leverton living room.

If, in his imagination, he cluttered the floor with electric cables and added a few floodlights to the books and pictures all round him, he could see what it really was – a kind of film set permanently ready for its star. Actually, it was a lot of fun. Or it would have been if Fliss and Rio stopped bickering. There was no sign of them letting up. 'We should have told him,' Rio insisted with a snarl.

'I don't agree.'

'Why not?'

'You know why not. I've explained it over and over again. Mr Emmett needs peace and quiet to get his work done. Also, these days, he can paint without any interruptions. It'll freak him out when he discovers the star of his favourite soap has moved in next door.'

'He might think it's an honour.'

'But he's a hermit, practically. For him, Rosie Ramone is someone to meet on screen not in real life.'

'Not for much longer – meeting her on screen, I mean.'

'So what's the point of telling him now? Let's leave him to his dreams, Rio. Denzel, what's your opinion?' Fliss was taking a chance and she knew it.

So did Denzel. Up till then, a combination of shrugs and sniffs and silences had kept him clear of the argument. Now, with both of them staring him out, he had to commit.

Cautiously, he nodded. 'I hear what you're saying,' he said. 'In fact, I've been hearing it for the last couple of days on and off. It's certainly time we settled it one way or the other.'

'Well, then?' said Rio.

His eyes had gone cold.

It was as if a vacancy had just opened up in the best friend department and maybe Denzel needn't bother to reapply.

Denzel sighed and turned to Fliss. 'I suppose, in the end, I'm with you on this. But you've got another reason for keeping Mr E in the dark, haven't you.'

'Another reason?'

'I reckon you know what I mean.'

'Yes, I do ...' said Fliss, blushing.

'Well, I don't,' said Rio. 'What are you both on about? Will somebody let me in on the secret?'

'It's not a secret, Rio. It's something I don't like to admit even to myself. The reason I want to keep things as they are with Mr Emmett is simply that – to keep things as they are. Once he knows we're Rosie Ramone's children, everything will change. Okay, so maybe he's bound to find out who Mum is eventually. But I'd like to keep things ordinary – to be a normal, everyday neighbour – for as long as I possibly can.'

'Fliss, things have never been normal for us.'

'Nor for your mum,' said Denzel. 'Being a superstar is all she knows. That's another reason to keep quiet. How would you like to have the Number One Fan of INSIDERS living next door when you're about to be dumped from the series?' This wasn't a happy thought.

Fliss and Rio slumped a little lower where they sat. Tactfully, Denzel went back to his survey of this weird and wonderful living space. For him, it was such a strange mixture of the stylish and the utterly messy that pretty nearly anything seemed to fit in here somewhere – even that bulging sack which had been propped against the end of the sofa. 'What's that?' he asked, curiously.

'Mum's fan mail,' said Rio.

'She puts it all in a sack does she?'

'No, that's how it arrives. She gets a couple of special deliveries from the post office every week. Mind you, since she held her press conference, it's been more like a sack every day. She's upstairs with her secretary now. They're still finishing the last batch.'

'Your mum answers every letter?'

'Well, every letter gets a reply. Usually, it's the same reply adapted a bit. Even so, it takes her hours.'

'Didn't she say there's been a flood of emails as well?'

Rio shrugged, helplessly. 'Stacks of them, Den. And the website has never had so many hits. The INSIDERS office is dealing with those, thank goodness. Serves them right, too. Almost all the callers want Mum to continue in the series.'

'So do most of the people who've written in to the newspapers or spoken on radio phone-ins,' said Fliss. 'Practically no one wants her written out.'

'And they'll still get rid of her?'

'Den, just watch them. These people can't bear to be wrong, remember. They'll argue that all the present uproar is the result of their brilliant campaign to stir up interest. It's a publicity triumph, they'll say – and that's all the more reason to ditch Rosie.'

'That's the stupidest thing I ever heard!'

'Not to them, it isn't. The more complaints they get about axing Rosie, the bigger the audience will be at Easter when everyone switches on to see if she really does get the chop.'

'So there's nothing at all that can save her?'

Rio and Fliss looked blank. It was hard to keep any hope alive on a gloomy afternoon like this. Already, more than two hours before teatime, the sun was hidden by clouds and the light beginning to fade. Then, from out in the hall, they heard the rattle of the letter box and a faint thud on the doormat. 'Post?' said Fliss, in surprise. 'At this time of the day?'

'Probably a pizza menu,' said Rio, standing up. 'Or some guff about double glazing.'

But when he returned, he was holding a postcard. 'It's from Mr Emmett, I think. Delivered by hand.'

'What's it say?'

'It's an invitation – to all three of us. Look, there's a sketch of our faces in the corner. And it's signed with the initials JKE. He wants us to come to something called a "private view" at three o'clock sharp this afternoon.'

'A private view of my portrait?'

'I suppose so, Fliss. What else could it be?'

'I bet he's just finished it,' said Denzel. 'That's about three days work, altogether – and another ten thousand quid in the bank. It takes my mum and dad six months to earn that much. If you ask me, this painting lark is a right scam.'

'Except it isn't three days.'

'Isn't it?'

Fliss shook her head. 'You're paying him for a lifetime of standing in front of an easel till he got it right. That's what Ms Marshall would say, I'm sure. Also he's still got to find a buyer, remember.'

'Yeah,' Rio grinned. 'And that may not be so easy considering it's a picture of you!'

CHAPTER 9

They were wrong about one aspect of the private view. It wasn't in Mr Emmett's studio at all. Instead, when they arrived at his front gate on the dot of three o'clock, he was waiting for them in the porch. 'He's dressed to go out,' Rio exclaimed.

'And he's got the picture with him,' said Denzel. 'Where's he taking us, I wonder?'

'It's lucky we've got our coats,' Fliss said.

Mr Emmett lifted his hand in greeting. He wore a long, old-fashioned mackintosh with a battered trilby hat pulled low over his eyes – like a spy perhaps, or a detective, in the sort of black and white movie that's only shown on television off-peak. 'Bless you for being on time, kids,' he said. 'I know it's rather short notice but I was sure you wouldn't let me down.'

'Thanks for the invitation,' said Denzel. 'We wouldn't want to miss out on a private view … wherever it is.'

'We're visiting an old friend of mine,' the old man explained. 'It's someone I haven't seen in quite a while, I'm sorry to say. I hope the three of you don't mind a bus ride. I'll take care of the tickets, of course … but I'd be grateful for some help with the painting. I'd forgotten how awkward they are to carry.'

'No problem,' Rio said. 'We're experts at that, Mr E. The three of us will take turns if you like.'

'Thank you, son.' Nervously, Mr Emmett looked at the sky.

Already it had started to rain.

So, for the second time that week, the bus they caught at the corner was crowded with passengers. Mr Emmett struggled on first to pay their fares, followed by Fliss and Rio. Denzel came last with the picture tucked under his arm. The driver eyed it, suspiciously. 'What's that thing?' he growled. 'This is a public vehicle, kid. You can't bring a parcel like that on a public vehicle.'

'Why not?' Denzel asked.

'It's the wrong sort of size for a start. And I don't like the look of those sticking-out corners.'

'All corners do that,' said Denzel.

'Not on my bus they don't. They could be a danger to other passengers in the event of a sudden emergency.'

'That's ordinary corners, mister.'

'Ordinary corners?'

'These corners aren't ordinary at all. They've been specially made. All four of them are collapsible.'

'Collapsible corners?' scoffed the driver. 'What kind of corner is that may I ask?'

'One that's designed for transportation,' Denzel said. 'On public vehicles which might be subject to a sudden emergency. It removes any danger to other passengers.'

The driver's mouth dropped open.

Then he started to laugh. 'Get on with you, kid. The cheek of the devil, you've got!'

Denzel had already passed the package to Rio and Fliss who'd been doing their best not to snigger out loud.

Now, even Mr Emmett and some other passengers were smiling. As they disembarked in the city centre, Rio had a fit of the giggles. 'That was wicked, Denzel,' he spluttered. 'You were making the whole thing up!'

'So was he, wasn't he?'

'Yes, but suppose there really had been a sudden emergency? What would you have done then?'

'Collapse, probably.' This set both of them off again.

The boys were still grinning, collapsing into puddles on the pavement, and pretending to be a danger to other pedestrians – with Fliss and Mr Emmett trying to ignore them – all the way to the gallery in the high street which had once been a greengrocer's shop.

Where else would they have been going, after all?

It was the only possible place to mark the comeback of Mr JK Emmett … assuming the old man kept his nerve. Up close, he stared balefully at the gallery's tinted window and trim, glossy paintwork. When he saw the seascape on display, he pulled out his handkerchief and dabbed at his brow. As Rio pushed open the heavy plate-glass door to usher him forward, his confidence faltered completely. 'Look,' he said, pulling the brim of his hat even lower over his face. 'Maybe this isn't such a good idea ...'

'Come on, Mr E,' said Fliss. Gently, she steered him inside.

The door hushed discreetly shut behind them.

Mr Emmett blinked at the art all around him. It was as if he expected a critic, dripping with cleverness, to leap out and stab him with a well turned phrase. 'Listen,' he began again. 'I really don't think we should go on with ...'

'Hello, Jim,' said Ms Marshall, stepping forward. Her delight that he'd come was obvious.

She wore a dove-grey suit today with a blouse that was blossomy pink. Even her nametag matched the change. She held out a hand in welcome.

'Since meeting your young friends here,' she said, 'I've been half-expecting you to drop in. It's really good to see you again. Have you got something there for me to look at?'

'Hello, Louise. Er … only this.'

'Another wonderful picture of the city centre?'

'No, this is a portrait. Well, it's a kind of portrait anyway. Young Fliss here has been helping me get it right. That's if I really have managed to get the thing right, mind you …'

'Modest as ever, Jim!'

Mr Emmett blushed.

Denzel offered her the parcel. 'Better undo it as carefully as last time, miss,' he warned. 'You never know, we may have to take it back on the bus. That taxi you paid for to get us home turned out to be a bit of a disaster. It drove off with the other picture, you see. We haven't seen a trace of it since!'

'It drove off with the …'

The gallery's Director of Acquisitions had gone white.

'He's only joking,' Rio said.

'Denzel's got a great sense of humour,' Fliss told her. 'But it does take a bit of getting used to.'

'So I recall,' Ms Marshall said. She gave Denzel a cool stare.

Then stuck out her tongue.

Denzel was so astonished, he almost dropped the parcel as he handed it over. Ms Marshall already had it safe, though. She laid it flat on the same desk as before, angled the same spotlight over it, and picked up the same stubby knife to cut away the packaging. It was as if no time had passed at all since their first visit to the gallery. As she pushed away the wrapping paper, she heard Mr Emmett's gentle cough. 'Stand it on its long side, please,' he said.

Ms Marshall looked at him quizzically but did as he asked.

All four of them stared at the painting. None of them had actually uttered a sound, but somehow a gasp of surprise seemed to be echoing round the room.

It wasn't a single portrait at all.

What they saw on the canvas was a trio
of pictures, like a strip cartoon, each the size
and shape of a television screen. Three faces
gazed out at the onlookers: Fliss on the left,
Rosie Ramone in the middle, and to the
right – fading off into the background like a
movie-style 'dissolve' – someone who could
have been either. 'I thought I'd call it, *Now
You See Her* … said Mr Emmett.

'… and now you don't,' whispered Fliss.

'Exactly, my dear.' He nodded,
thoughtfully.

His hair was spiky with rain where he'd taken off his hat. This he twisted nervously in his hands, scattering tiny beads of water on the rich, plush carpet. 'Without you, Fliss, I wouldn't have seen her at all – not as the subject of a picture, anyway. But you do look so uncannily like a young Rosie Ramone, you know.'

'I know,' Fliss said.

'With your face to get me started, and the help of Mother's videos, the painting seemed to be waiting for me – there on the canvas. All I needed to do was uncover it with my brush.'

They could see that. The three-in-one portrait was as fresh and clear and childlike as his vision of the city centre.

There was a rustle of stiff, damp raincoat as Mr Emmett shuffled his feet uncomfortably. 'I owe a debt to Rosie Ramone, you see. If she hadn't kept Mother amused with every new episode of INSIDERS, not to mention constantly replaying the tapes, I'd never have had the freedom to go on painting. So when Fliss suddenly dropped in on me shortly before the news broke that Rosie was being axed from the series … well, I felt a little tribute was in order.' He crooked his head at the portrait.

Then, as if satisfied with what he saw, he straightened up in a way that was almost defiant. 'This canvas was painted mainly for me, I must admit. So please don't worry if it's not the kind of thing you're looking for as the gallery's Director of Acquisitions, Louise. I'll quite understand if you think it's too … well, *personal*.'

'Personal?' said Ms Marshall. She shook herself as if she'd been lost in a dream.

Was it the painting that held her attention or simply a reluctance to disappoint Mr Emmett?

Her eyes narrowed. 'Too personal, eh?' she murmured. 'Well, it's easy enough to run a check on that one – with these neighbours of yours, for instance, assuming they're fans of INSIDERS. Are you two as horrified as I am by what's happening to Rosie Ramone?'

'You bet,' said Rio.

'We certainly are,' agreed Fliss.

'And how about you?'

'It's a scandal,' Denzel responded at

once. 'They should be strung up by their thumbs, those TV bosses.'

'My opinion in a nutshell,' said Ms Marshall. 'I even watch the omnibus edition at weekends – along with millions of other INSIDERS addicts, I expect. If this portrait is personal, Jim, then in my estimate it's personal for half the nation at the very least!'

'You like it, then?'

'Jim, it's superb. Also it's totally original. What other major living painter has dared celebrate the fleeting nature of television as you've done here?'

'Yeah …' said Denzel.

'But there's much more to it than that. *Now You See Her* … is true, blisteringly true. It's also an eye-opener. We're seeing someone like Rosie for the very first time, I feel. But she's also fading as we look – slowly but surely – as we all do  in the end, however hard we try to pretend otherwise. Unless I'm very much mistaken, this picture will stun everyone who sees it.'

Denzel laid a hand on Mr Emmett's arm. 'Trust me on this,' he said. 'I think she definitely likes it.'

Fliss and Rio definitely liked it, too. What was the word he'd used ... a tribute?

There were worse ways than this to show Mum saying goodbye to being a superstar, it seemed to them – even if Mr Emmett's particular way did bring teasing glances from Denzel. They almost sighed with relief when Ms Marshall suggested leaving the business details till later. 'That needn't delay us from reminding everyone who you are, Jim,' she said. 'We can get started immediately by giving your picture pride of place in the gallery.'

'You're really sure, Louise?'

'I'm absolutely positive. It won't be in our window long, in any case. There's one admirer of yours I can think of straightaway who'll be very interested in this ...' Already she was reaching for her security keys.

Altering the window display took rather longer than they expected what with shutting off the entire alarm system and sliding back the thick, thief-proof glass mounted in stainless-steel runners. It was like opening a huge, see-through strongbox.

Ms Marshall, helped by one of her assistants, clambered into the window herself to change the paintings over. Once Mr Emmett's canvas was in position, and the lighting adjusted accordingly, she left the assistant to rearrange the velvet drapes. 'If this masterpiece doesn't make shoppers, buskers, traffic wardens and all other passers-by stop dead in their tracks,' she said, beaming, 'then my name's Vincent Van Gogh ... or maybe it's JK Emmett!'

Outside, it was raining steadily now. So crossing the road to the teashop opposite called for a sharp eye on the traffic as well as coat collars turned up high against the downpour. What with the glitter of reflected light on the road surface, and the lowering clouds above, the city centre looked more than ever like a scene painted by JK Emmett. Ms Marshall was determined they should have a treat, though. 'If any kids deserve a few sticky buns or a couple of chocolate eclairs, then it's you lot,' she insisted.

'You can say that again,' Mr Emmett nodded.

'Fine by us,' grinned Rio. 'Assuming you can find any empty seats on a day like this.'

They got the last available table in the teashop. It was just inside, as it happened, where the draught from the doorway was gustiest. The whole room felt damp and steamy, especially near the window itself. Raindrops blurred their view of the high street even more. On the far pavement, the spotlights in the gallery glimmered brightly as if from some sea-going vessel trapped temporarily in the shallows.

'You can still see Mr E's picture, though,' said Denzel, wiping the windowpane with the back of his hand. 'And you can see loads of people staring at it as well!'

'In weather like this?' said Ms Marshall, sharply.

'Have a look if you don't believe me.'
But Denzel was right.

Already, at least a dozen shoppers were jostling each other for the best place to view Rosie's picture.

Soon, the crowd that had gathered was spilling into the road.

Above the umbrellas, the rainhoods, the plastic hats and even a few folded newspapers, the portrait of Rosie Ramone glowed like a ship's beacon.

Fliss, Rio and Denzel shook their heads in amazement – while continuing to pay due attention to their buns and chocolate eclairs. Perhaps embarrassed by all the fuss, Mr Emmett only picked at his. Ms Marshall, on the other hand, ignored every cake on her plate.

She was talking rapidly into her mobile phone.

CHAPTER 10

After that, thanks to Ms Marshall's canny stage management, everything fell neatly into place. The camera teams arrived while the crowd was at its thickest, and the rain at its heaviest, and there was a pleasing number of reporters from the local press and radio. 'We'll catch the evening news if we're lucky,' Ms Marshall said. 'By tomorrow all the talk shows will be on to us.'

'Talk shows?'

'Don't worry, Jim. I'll take care of them.' Ms Marshall could take care of anything, apparently.

That's how it seemed to Denzel, anyway. 'She's brilliant,' he declared the next day. 'She had everything sorted before you could wash out a paintbrush!'

'Or price up a portrait,' said Rio. 'Remember, if Mr E's picture is a success, she stands to gain as well.'

'What about Mum?' Fliss asked.

'Mum?'

'Maybe she stands to gain, too ...'

Rio and Denzel exchanged a glance. They hadn't thought of that. Could this be the evidence they needed that Rosie

Ramone really was worth preserving as a national treasure? No … surely not. You can't change the mind of someone like Hal McRory, Head of Series Drama at a multi-million pound TV company, with a bit of milling about in the rain outside a provincial art gallery.

Or can you?

Maybe you can when the gallery in question has been a feature of every front page, airwave, bus queue, commuter train and over-the-fence conversation throughout the entire country since the news first broke. They'd lost count of how many times they'd come across an appearance by Ms Marshall as they hopped between channels and stations. By now, they knew parts of her spiel by heart:

'What other major living painter …'
'… seeing someone like Rosie for the very first time …'
'… true, blisteringly true …'
'… It's also an eye-opener …'
'… celebrate the fleeting nature of television …'
'… this portrait will stun everyone who sees it.'

Denzel was lost in admiration. 'Just listen to her!' he hooted. 'If you hear it often enough, said in exactly the same words, you've got to believe it makes sense!'

'But it does make sense,' said Rio.

'Complete sense,' Fliss added.

'Yeah …' said Denzel. That was the bit that baffled him.

Twice this morning, they'd slipped out into the garden to take a peek at Mr Emmett's window. They'd stood there for as long as they could bear it. The upstairs room was empty as far as they could tell. In Fliss' opinion, he was lying low while the worst of the uproar passed. According to Rio, he was probably playing some of Mother's INSIDERS tapes in the sitting room at the front of the house.

Denzel didn't much care what the old man was up to. With the sky overhead an icy blue, and a sharp northerly wind rattling the trees in the surrounding gardens, all he wanted was to scuttle indoors again where it wasn't so cold.

It was toasty warm back in the living room.

All this showbiz stuff on the walls was

definitely beginning to grow on him, Denzel decided. One day, maybe, he'd join the INSIDERS team himself. Then again, he wouldn't mind being some kind of painter in a ramshackle studio like Mr Emmett's. That's if he wasn't tempted to follow in the footsteps of Ms Marshall and become a top executive in the art world. Life was full of possibilities.

Also it was full of surprises.

All three of them, for instance – Fliss and Rio as much as Denzel – were astonished when Mum finally came downstairs. She slipped into the room absent-mindedly, almost shyly, still in her dressing gown. Under her arm was a pile of newspapers. 'Good day to you, family,' she said in a faraway voice. 'Good day to you, young friend.'

'Hello, Mum.'

'Hello, Mrs … er … Leverton.'

'Rosie is quite sufficient, dear,' she said, smiling sweetly. She settled herself gracefully on the sofa.

They watched as she riffled through the papers. She seemed to be looking at anything – anything at all – apart from the

lead story in every one of them. How could
she possibly miss something that shrieked
look at me, look at me quite so blatantly? Or
did she know exactly what she was doing as
she skimmed the sports reports, the business
section, the letters column ... any printed
page on offer, it seemed, except those
clamouring hardest for her attention?

At last, Rio had had enough. 'Mum?' he
said, sharply.

'Yes, my darling?'

Rio rolled his eyes at the others. 'Mum, have you had any phone calls today by any chance?'

'Phone calls, darling?'

'Phone calls, Mum. Where you pick up a handset and there's someone at the other end who wants to talk to you.'

'Oh, phone calls ...'

'Those things, yes. A ringing sound, remember? And after that – if you've pressed the right button – words flying to and fro. It's quite a popular means of communication nowadays.'

'There's no need for sarcasm, darling.'

'Isn't there?' said Rio.

With great care, as if each and every one of them were a priceless ancient manuscript, Mum laid her newspapers aside. Elegantly, she took off her glasses. 'As it happens, darling, I have had a couple of phone conversations this morning. One was from Miriam, my agent. It seems there's been a re-think about my new INSIDERS contract – it's now a lifetime contract, actually. Then I spoke to my dear, dear friend Hal McRory ...'

'The guy who's just sacked you,' Rio reminded her.

'Sacked me? Oh, no … not any more. That was just an unfortunate misunderstanding. It was a decision that should never have been made, he told me. You can't imagine the fuss and bother it's caused. The fact is, they were already considering a complete rethink when this painting business cropped up …'

'Painting business?' said Fliss.

'Well, I've only got Hal's word for the details. But it seems there's a highly distinguished artist – living somewhere in this very neighbourhood, he says – who's just exhibited a marvellous portrait of me. It's in some gallery close to the city centre.'

'Mum, what's that got to do with …?'

'Darling, please don't interrupt! By a strange coincidence, the chairman of the company that makes INSIDERS happens to be a great admirer of this man's pictures. He's been collecting them for years. So he's desperate to see this one hanging in the company boardroom. Hal's been instructed to buy it at once.'

'How much for?' asked Denzel, sitting up.

'Oh, thousands and thousands of pounds – the woman at the gallery is an absolute terror, apparently. She was on the phone to the chairman soon after the portrait was brought to her. I'm told the story is in all the newspapers though I haven't been able to find it.'

'Try the front page,' Fliss grinned.

'The front page, darling? Oh, surely not … that's the most important page in the paper! Anyway, the outcome as far as I'm concerned is that it's back to the treadmill. I'm a permanent fixture in the schedules now. Rosie Ramone and INSIDERS have got me trapped forever, darlings …'

Mum lifted a weary hand to her brow.

Straightaway, Rio did the same – followed closely by Fliss and Denzel. 'Trapped forever, darlings!' they intoned. After this, they collapsed in a giggling heap.

Mum stared at them haughtily for a while. She was doing her best to look offended but even she couldn't keep it up for long. Bit by bit, her face split into the widest of grins. As she joined in their laughter herself, the newspapers slid to the floor in a small avalanche of newsprint. 'Forever, darlings!' she whooped at the top of her voice. 'They've signed me up forever!' Being an actor, she could whoop pretty loudly, too.

If it hadn't been for the thickness of the walls, the double glazing on every window, and having his hearing aid switched off, Mr Emmett might have heard her up in his room next door.